British Library Cataloguing in Publication Data
Hayes, Barbara
  Adventure on the Water.—(A Town and Country
  Mouse Story)
  I. Title   II. Mendoza, Phillip   III. Series
  813′.54[J]    PZ7

ISBN 0 216 92033 7

Blackie and Son Limited
7 Leicester Place
London WC2H 7BP

Printed in Belgium

# Adventure on the Water

Barbara Hayes
Illustrated by Phillip Mendoza

**Blackie**

**O**ne hot summer's morning Mr Badger the postman found Flora paddling in the river.

"Good morning," called Mr Badger. "There's a letter for you at your house."

"A letter!" cried Flora. "How exciting. I love surprises! I wonder who it's from?"

"Well, it was posted in the town," said Mr Badger. "It must be from your cousin, Annabel."

"I said I liked *surprises*!" laughed Flora.

"But you don't know what's in it yet, so it's still a surprise," said Mr Badger. "Let's go and see . . ."

They walked up the lane to Flora's cottage, while Mr Badger told Flora about what thirsty work it was delivering letters.

"You'd better come in and have a drink, then," said Flora kindly when they reached her front door.

"It *is* from Annabel," said Flora, opening the letter.

"I knew it," said Mr Badger, triumphantly. Flora knew she would have to tell him what the letter said. Mr Badger always had to know everything.

"Annabel and Jeremy are coming to visit us," said Flora, reading the letter. "They're coming by steamboat . . . and . . . Oh my! They'll be here today!"

And indeed at that moment Annabel and Jeremy were leaving town.

The two smart town mice drove to the riverbank where they boarded a grand steamboat.

"How delightful!" exclaimed Annabel as the boat slowly made its way down river.

But then the wind caught her hat, whisked it into the air and dropped it right down in the water! The captain had to stop the boat while a helpful fisherman rescued it. Poor Annabel felt very foolish. She could hear the other passengers laughing at her. She decided she did not like steamers.

"Jeremy," she said. "Steamboats are noisy and smelly! We must hire a nice quiet punt. Hurry up, Flora and Fred will be waiting!"

But punting wasn't easy, as Jeremy found out. "How do you turn corners?" he cried. "Oh no! How do you stop —"

Crunch! The punt crashed into the riverbank spilling Annabel and Jeremy into the water.

Fortunately, Flora and Fred heard their cries for help.

"Look!" Fred pointed, laughing. "Annabel and Jeremy have arrived at last — in a shipwreck!"

"Oh dear!" said Flora. "Annabel will be furious!"

Flora and Fred jumped into their little boat and rowed over to Annabel and Jeremy.

"Let's jump up and down," Jeremy suggested brightly. "We'll soon dry off!"

"That's a silly idea," said Annabel, who was feeling cross and bedraggled. "Fred, you must row us over to that big house on the other side of the river. Whoever lives there is sure to have some nice spare clothes."

Fred and Flora felt rather nervous knocking on the door of such a grand house. But a small, kindly mouse answered and invited them all in.

While Annabel and Jeremy's clothes were drying they all sat in front of a blazing fire and Annabel told the little mouse all about her adventures.

"I don't think I like boats or rivers any more," she declared. "I wish we had gone to the seaside instead."

"Well," said the little mouse. "It isn't far to the seaside. Why don't you stay here tonight and drive there tomorrow?"

"What a lovely idea," cried Flora. "Fred and I will come too."

"But how will you get there?" asked Annabel. "There isn't room for us all in the car."

"Oh, in a rowing boat of course," said Flora.

Early next morning Flora and Fred set off in their rowing boat. Jeremy was up early, too, to fetch the car. It was a lovely day, but the wind was quite strong. Annabel held on tightly to her hat all the way.

At the seaside Jeremy went to look for Flora and Fred, but they were nowhere to be found.

The stiff breeze had blown their boat out to sea and no matter how hard Fred rowed, he could not get any nearer the shore.

Then Fred's hat blew away. "That will teach you to laugh at Annabel," giggled Flora.

Luckily, Jeremy knew exactly what to do. He called the coastguard.

"Oh Jeremy!" cried Annabel, as they watched the little boat being towed in. "You are wonderful. I'm so proud that you helped rescue our cousins."

"I always wanted a trip round the lighthouse," said Flora, once she and Fred were safely ashore.

But secretly she agreed with Annabel that they should all spend the rest of the holiday on the beach — and keep well away from the water!